For anyone who can never have enough cats

—N.R.

For Lou and Sarah

—J.J.

Bruno, the Standing Cat

Nadine Robert
& Jean Jullien

Random House New York

One morning, just as Peter was about to butter his toast, he heard a mewing sound at the window.

"The neighbor's cat must be hungry," he said to himself.

But the meows soon changed into insistent cries, so Peter got up to see what was going on.

When he opened the door, the meows stopped! Peter found a box with a name written on it—*Bruno.*

So he decided to open it.

Free at last, Bruno the cat
rose up on his back legs.

"Gee, Bruno! You're standing!"

Peter had never seen a cat stand up,
but that didn't matter. He had always
wanted a cat.

So Peter adopted Bruno.

One day after school, Pam came over
to Peter's house.
"Hey, do you want to play outside?"

Pam tagged along when Peter
and Bruno ran to the park.

"But . . . how did you teach your cat to do that?" asked Pam.

"I didn't teach him," answered Peter. "He could always do that. Bruno is a standing cat."

"Oh, wow! Can Bruno catch mice?"

"No, but he loves to chase
them on his skateboard."

"Awesome! Does Bruno like
to play with balls of yarn?"

"No, but he loves to play house and serve me tea."

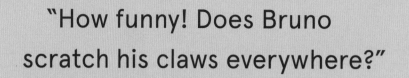

"How funny! Does Bruno
scratch his claws everywhere?"

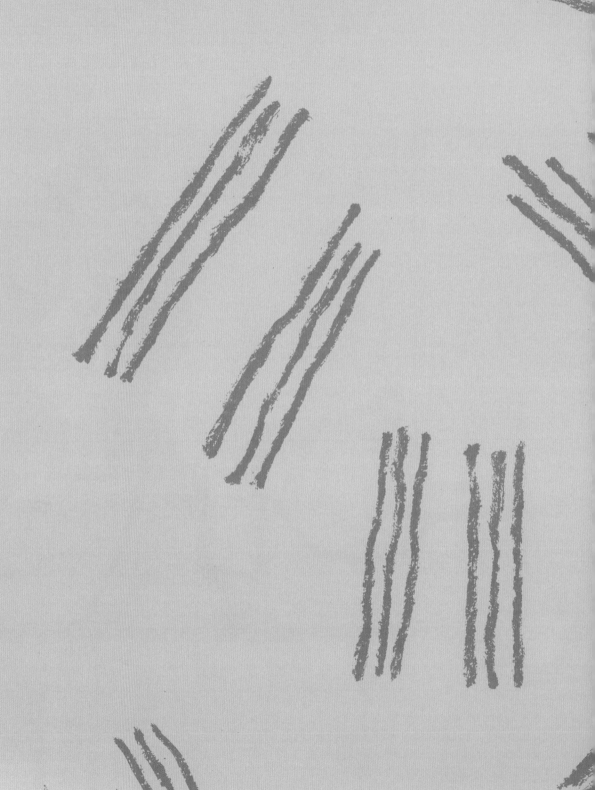

"No, never. But sometimes
he likes to give me a back rub."

"Lucky you. Does Bruno
eat regular cat food?"

"No, he won't eat it. But he does like chewing bubble gum. He can even blow bubbles upside down."

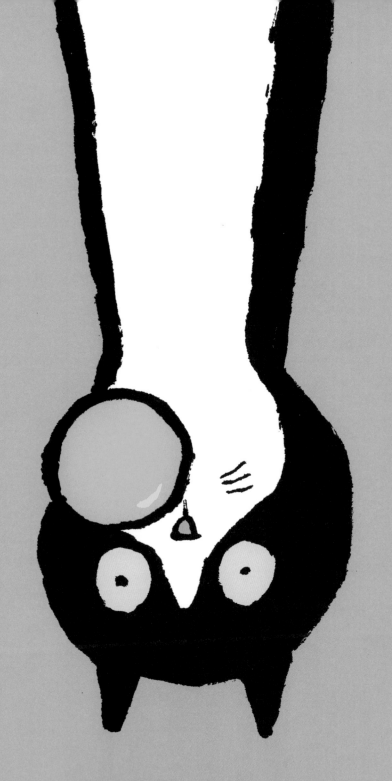

"Amazing! Does he like to hide in his box?"

"No, not at all. But you should see
him when he hears his favorite song!"

"Yeah, not bad! Can Bruno do
something that nobody else can do?"
"Watch this!"

Bruno starts to run . . .

. . . he flies . . .

. . . and he catches the ball!

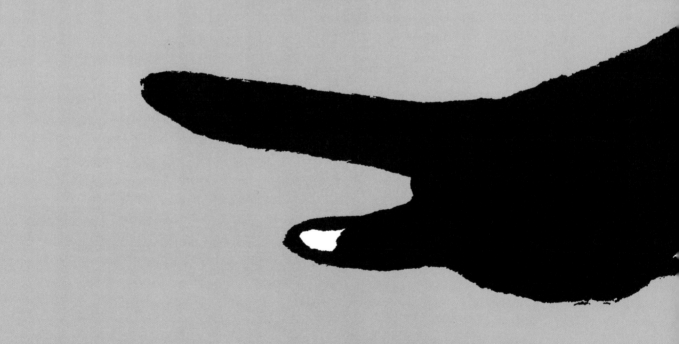

"WHOOPIE!" exclaims Pam.

"Bruno is a standing cat and he is unique. But what I like the most . . .

". . . is that he is my friend!"